Curious George DISCOVERS

Germs

Adaptation by Erica Zappy

Based on the TV series teleplay
written by Peter Hirsch

Houghton Mifflin Harcourt

Boston   New York

Photograph on cover (top right) courtesy of MVA Scientific Consultants

Photographs on cover (top left and bottom) and pp. 4, 13, 30, 32 (bottom) courtesy of HMH/Carrie Garcia

Photograph on p. 14 © Sharon Hoogstraten Photography/Houghton Mifflin Harcourt

Photograph on p. 20 © Eric Camden/Houghton Mifflin Harcourt

All other photographs © Houghton Mifflin Harcourt

For information about permission to reproduce selections from this book, write to Permissions, Houghton Mifflin Harcourt Publishing Company, 215 Park Avenue South, New York, New York 10003.

ISBN: 978-0-544-45422-4 paper over board
ISBN: 978-0-544-43066-2 paperback

Design by Susanna Vagt
www.hmhco.com
Printed in China
SCP 10 9 8 7 6 5 4 3 2 1
4500515629

George is a good little monkey, and always very curious. But sometimes even good little monkeys find themselves not feeling so well. How did George know he was sick? The story starts with spaghetti sauce!

George's favorite day of the week was Sauce Day at Chef Pisghetti's restaurant. He always gave Chef Pisghetti some tips to make the best sauce. But today, instead of being able to taste the chef's new Molto Jolto sauce, George couldn't taste anything!

Chef Pisghetti sent George home, and the man with the yellow hat sent George to bed. Then, he took George's temperature.

"Fever. Stuffy nose. Clammy paws," said the man. "You are definitely fighting a germ, George."

Do you know what a germ is? George was curious.

The man got out a book. There was a picture of a funny-looking blob. "This is a bad germ, George. There are good germs and bad germs. A bad germ is making you sick," the man explained. "Germs are very small. They can be found anywhere in your body: your nose, your mouth, your stomach, your lungs. But that's enough biology for today. Tired monkeys need their rest."

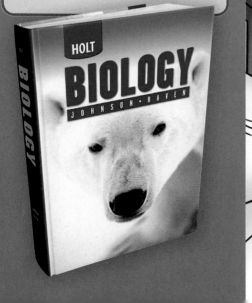

George might have been sick, but he was still curious. Where did the germ come from? And more important, how could he get rid of it? He was still wondering when he dozed off . . .

Soon George was dreaming. In his dream he was very small . . . like a germ! He and his pal Gnocchi were going to take a trip inside George's sleeping body to fight off the bad germs!

Did you know . . .

The man with the yellow hat said that some germs are good and some are bad. That means that in your body right now are some bacteria, or germs, that help your body instead of making you sick. Good germs can help make vitamins that your body needs. You can even get some of these good bacteria by eating favorite foods such as yogurt and cheese!

George and Gnocchi zoomed into sleeping George's mouth and landed right on his tongue. It was soft and squishy. And there was music playing! They hadn't expected that! What could it be? It seemed to be coming from his nose.

When George and Gnocchi got to the nose, they saw a funny-looking blob strumming a guitar and singing!

"I'll make you sniff and I'll make you sneeze,
You won't be smelling that smelly cheese!
We'll be making you sweat and making you squirm,
Because that's how germs are being germs!"

George could hardly believe his eyes.

"I'm Toots, the singing germ," he introduced himself, "and these are my backup singers, the Germettes."

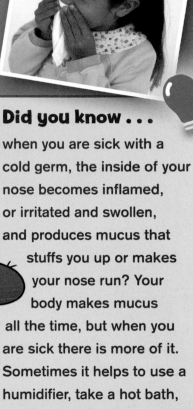

Did you know . . .

when you are sick with a cold germ, the inside of your nose becomes inflamed, or irritated and swollen, and produces mucus that stuffs you up or makes your nose run? Your body makes mucus all the time, but when you are sick there is more of it. Sometimes it helps to use a humidifier, take a hot bath, and drink a lot of fluids.

FRESH

Orange Juice

0% Real Juice

(2 QT) 1.89L • Pasteurized

Seeing Toots in his nose made George upset. He wanted that germ out of him!

But Toots did not want to go. In fact, he took the Germettes and headed to George's lungs, laughing and singing all the way.

George and Gnocchi chased the germs to the lungs. George noticed that when the lungs got smaller, air went out. And when the lungs got bigger, a rush of air came in. He was watching himself breathe!

Test it out!

Put your hand just above your bellybutton. Take a deep breath in. Do you feel your tummy get bigger? That's because your lungs are filling up with air. Now breathe all the way out. What happens then? Try breathing fast or very slow. See how your body changes when you do this.

George's lungs gave him an idea. He remembered something he saw in the germ book: coughing and sneezing are the lungs' way of doing their job and trying to force out bad germs. All George had to do was sneeze Toots right out of his body!

George and Gnocchi chased Toots and the Germettes all the way to George's nose. Then, with one big sneeze (thanks to some well-positioned tickling) out went Toots and the Germettes . . . out into the air, looking for a new place to live.

A few days later, George was feeling much better. He had taken lots of naps, drunk lots of water and juice, and sneezed out those germs. He could even smell again! But it was clear where Toots and the Germettes had found a new home. George's friend the man with the yellow hat was sick!

The man had taken such good care of George when he was sick. Now George wanted to help his friend get better, too. So he made some soup.

George brought the soup to the man's bed.

"Thanks, George," the man said. But when he tried
the soup, he couldn't taste anything.

George wanted to taste it, but his friend stopped him.

"George, don't use that spoon! It might be covered with my cold germs. You don't want to get sick again, do you?" the man asked.

George definitely did not want to get sick again.

That made George curious. How else did germs get from one person to another? He looked at his germ book. George knew that the germs were in him just a few days ago, but his friend had not used George's spoon—or fork, or cup! Do you think the man caught George's germs when he sneezed or coughed?

Looking at the book made George sleepy. He drifted into
another dream—now he and Gnocchi were inside the man
with the yellow hat's body. There was that music again,
coming from the man's stomach. They needed to find Toots
so they could kick him out again!

"Well, I've been lots of places, floating free as a wheeze,
Riding on your silverware or flying on sleeves!
I played in many people all across this great big land,
Especially in the folks who don't like to wash their hands.
Because soap makes me wiggle, and soap makes me sneer,
One sign of soap, and this Toots is out of here!"

If George heard Toots correctly, getting his friend to wash his hands would be a good way to help him get rid of the germs and feel better.

But Toots and the Germettes remembered George, and knew they needed to get away from him. "We're off to play in another body," Toots said—they were going to infect someone else!

"Get ready to hop on that hand when he wipes his nose!" yelled Toots to his Germettes. George didn't want the germs inside his friend, but he didn't want anyone else to be sick either. He had to stop them.

When the bell rang and the man got up to answer the door, Toots and the Germettes were ready for a new body . . . Professor Wiseman's! She had also made soup for her sick friend.

George and Gnocchi zoomed out after the germs and landed with a thud on Professor Wiseman's hand. The germs were startled. "Oooh, it feels like something is crawling on my hands!" Professor Wiseman said.

"I should probably wash them inside."

Professor Wiseman went to the bathroom and washed Toots and the Germettes right down the drain!

Not only had George chased those germs out of his friend, he (and some soap) had stopped them from getting Professor Wiseman sick, too.

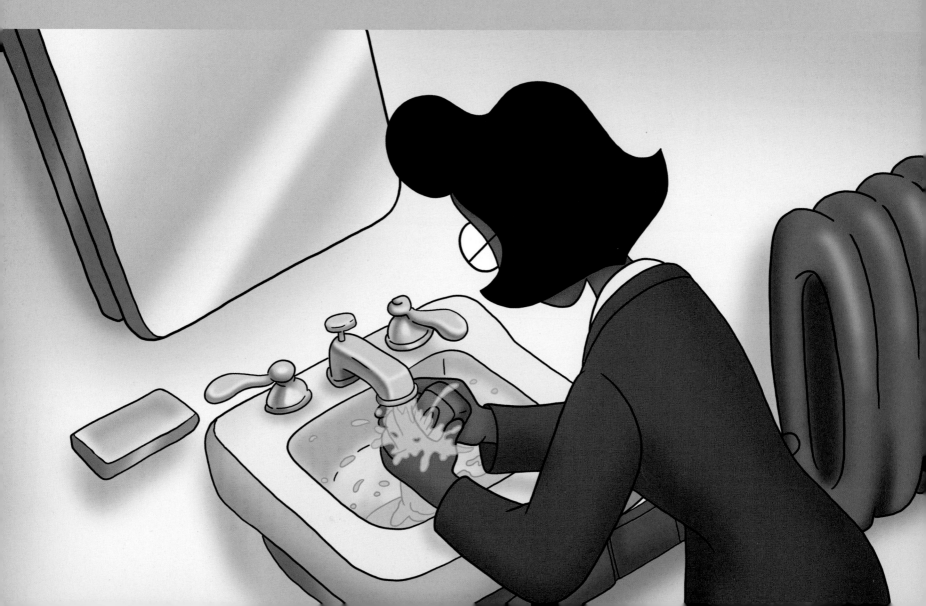

When George woke up from his dream, he felt great. But he went straight to the bathroom to wash his hands—and feet—just in case. After two icky adventures with Toots, this healthy little monkey wanted to stay that way!

Five-Second Rule

If you drop a piece of food on the ground, do you ever hear someone say, "Pick it up, quick! Five-second rule!" Often, people call out the five-second rule because they think that if you get food off the floor quickly enough, there won't be any germs on it. But did you know that scientists have done studies to show that even in less than five seconds, germs can make their way onto your food and into your body?

Try an experiment at home.
You'll need:

- two slices of fresh bread
- two zipper-lock bags
- a permanent marker

Directions:

First, wash your hands with soap and water. Place one slice of bread in a bag and close it tight, making sure to get all of the extra air out. Label this bag "A" with your marker.

Drop the other piece of bread flat onto the floor (in your kitchen, bathroom, on a rug, or even outside!). Leave the bread on the ground for five full seconds (count 1 Mississippi, 2 Mississippi . . .). Then place that piece of bread in the second bag. Don't forget to get all of the extra air out and zip it closed tight. Label this bag "B" so you remember which is which.

Check on your pieces of bread each day until mold begins to show. Did one piece get moldy more quickly, or in more places? Which one? What do you think happened?

Soup's on!

Does warm soup help you feel better when you are sick? Here's a yummy soup recipe (with or without chicken) that you and a grownup can prepare next time someone in your house is not feeling well.

Ingredients:

1 tablespoon vegetable oil

1 medium onion, chopped

2 carrots, chopped

2 stalks of celery, chopped

2 garlic cloves, minced

2 32-oz cartons of chicken or vegetable broth

2 cups chopped cooked chicken (optional)

1/4 teaspoon dried thyme

1/2 cup uncooked short pasta

Directions:

Heat oil in a saucepan over medium-high heat until hot.

Stir in onion, carrot, and celery and sauté for 5 minutes.

Add garlic and sauté one minute more until the vegetables are tender.

Stir in broth, chicken, and thyme, bringing the mixture to a boil.

Reduce heat and simmer, stirring occasionally, for 15 minutes. Add pasta and cook for 8 minutes, until pasta is tender.

To make this recipe vegetarian, simply use vegetable broth instead of chicken broth and leave out the chicken. You can also add other vegetables to make it heartier. Try adding a can of diced tomatoes in with the broth, or some fresh chopped spinach when the pasta goes in.

Healthy Habits

Wash up!

Make a list of times you and your family should wash your hands with soap and water, and post it on your refrigerator or in your bathroom.

Some ideas:
- **Before and after eating**
- **After using the bathroom**
- **After playing with animals, even your pets!**
- **Before and after visiting sick friends or family**
- **After you cough, sneeze, or blow your nose**
- **After playing outside**

You can sing a song to make sure you are washing your hands long enough to get rid of germs. A good one to try is "Happy Birthday"!

An Apple a Day

The old saying "an apple a day keeps the doctor away" may have some truth to it. That doesn't mean you'll never get sick if you eat an apple every day. But an apple has many great nutrients that help keep your body healthy, and eating apples regularly may make you healthier in the long run. Just be sure to eat the skin, too, since that's where most of the nutrients are!

It is always a good idea to eat a variety of fruits, vegetables, and whole grains for a well-balanced diet.

Explore further!

Eating right and washing your hands aren't the only ways to stay healthy (though they are important!).

Here are some ways you can stay healthy all year round:
- **Get enough rest (that means 10 hours of sleep a night!)**
- **Drink plenty of water**
- **Get lots of fresh air and exercise**
- **Dress appropriately for all weather**
- **Take a vitamin**
- **Visit the doctor regularly**